THE CHRONICLES OF GUS,

THE

GHOST-FACE DOG

SUSAN MITCHELL

Updated 1-21-2021

Dedication & Acknowledgements

This book is dedicated to my wonderful grandchildren, Ethan, Logan, and Elyssa, their parents Benjamin and Joy Mitchell, my grandchildren Cara and Calum, their parents Dave and Nichole Mitchell, my son Jacob Mitchell, and my beloved husband, David Mitchell.

I want to say a special thank you to my husband, David, for all his support and his contributions of knowledge and ideas. Also, I want to thank my sister-in-law, Alison Garner, who was my motivator and editor. Additionally, thank you to my father, Mack Garner, for his historical storytelling.

Table of Contents

Chapter 1

Chief Straight Arrow

Ethan and his brother, Logan, sister Elyssa, and their cousins, Cal and Cara, were all staying at their grandparents' ranch during their summer vacation. They had been hiking for a long time when they stopped at the ruins of an old pioneer homestead which Grandpa had told Ethan all about last summer.

The cabin had burned down many years ago. All the children gathered next to the ruins while Ethan began retelling the story which Grandpa had told him. Back in about 1860, there was a band from the Comanche tribe that lived in the area. Their leader was a wise warrior called Chief Straight Arrow, who allowed the pioneers to live there in peace. Ethan had learned the Comanche word for arrow is Pa'aka which sounded really cool to everyone.

Nimrod Hughes and his brother, Moses Hughes, were among the first pioneers to settle in the area and Nimrod was their direct ancestor. Nimrod means sharpshooter.

One morning, Chief Straight Arrow was on his way to trade with the pioneers, when he disappeared without a trace. The Comanches declared war on the pioneers because they thought the settlers had killed their chief. Many of the pioneers and Comanches were killed. The Texas Rangers finally had to step in and stop the uprising.

After Ethan told the story, the children exchanged ideas about what might have happened to the chief.

"I wonder what happened to Chief Straight Arrow," Logan said.

"Nobody knows," Ethan answered. "He just disappeared, and a lot of people were hurt for no reason."

"I wish we had lived back then. I bet we could have found some clues as to what happened," Logan stated. He remembered how they had all found the stolen bank loot in the Haunted Mansion and captured the bank robber with the help of their dogs.

"If we would have lived back then, we would have found Chief Straight Arrow and prevented the uprising," exclaimed Cal, and they all wished they could have been there.

The group chose to have their picnic close to the ruins. Grandma had fixed them a great lunch. They had grilled chicken, rolls, and corn on the cob with water, juice, and lemonade to drink. When they finished eating, they gave the leftovers to Gus and Luke. After such a long hike and eating so much of Grandma's wonderful lunch, Cara, Elyssa, and the boys were very tired. They made beds out of leaves and took a nap with their dogs sleeping beside them. When they woke up, they realized they were in a different time after they noticed the house next to them was in perfect shape.

"Wow! What is going on?" Cara exclaimed.

"Don't worry," Ethan said. "This has happened to me before. I went to sleep in the ruins and woke up in another time, but when I went back to sleep later, I woke back up in my own time."

"If that's the case, let's make the most of our day here," said Cal. Everyone agreed.

Ethan was thrilled. "I can't believe this has happened again and this time, Gus and I are not alone!"

A pioneer lady came out of the house. She was walking to the garden and stopped in surprise. "Hello there! Where did y'all come from?" she asked. She seemed very nice.

"Our family is camped along the creek a few miles from here," Ethan answered. "We are just exploring."

"Well, y'all are very welcome here, but the Comanches in this area are about to go on the war path. You had better warn your family!"

"What happened?" Elyssa asked.

"Their chief, Straight Arrow, is missing. His band of Comanches thinks we had something to do with his disappearance, but we didn't. They said he left early this morning, but he never arrived here."

"Do you know where he was last seen?" Logan asked.

"Not too far from here, by Lucy Creek. May I get y'all anything to eat or drink?"

"No thank you ma'am." Cara replied. "You have been very kind."

"Come back anytime!"

Cara, Elyssa, and the boys said goodbye, waved, and started walking toward Lucy Creek. When they got there, they found some of the pioneer kids fishing. One was a little girl that looked a lot like Cara.

The pioneer children and time travelers greeted each other, introducing themselves. The girl that looked like Cara was named Elizabeth.

"I really like your dogs," Elizabeth said.

"We sure have been catching a lot of catfish," one of the pioneer boys announced. "Y'all are welcome to come to our house for a catfish supper tonight."

Cara, Elyssa, and their brothers thanked the pioneer children for the invitation and said they would come if they could.

"We've got to take these fish home and finish our chores," the pioneer boy said. "I hope to see you again."

"I sure hope so," they all chimed in.

"Everyone is so nice and friendly here," Cara said after they left. "I wish we could stay here for a long time."

The other time travelers agreed.

"This might be our chance to prevent a war. We've got to find out what happened to Chief Straight Arrow!" Ethan stated.

"Maybe we should divide up," Logan suggested. "Cara, Cal, and Luke can go north along the creek. Ethan, Elyssa, Gus, and I can go south."

"Okay," Ethan agreed. "If we don't find anything in one hour, we'll meet back here. If the others are not at the meeting point, it means they found something and the rest of us will join them."

The kids checked their watches and started their search for Chief Straight Arrow and for any clues to his disappearance. After hiking for a while, Cara tripped over a tree stump that was sticking up a few inches out of the ground. When she fell, she twisted her ankle.

"Ouch! I can't walk right now," Cara said. "Go on ahead and let me rest for a while. I will wait right

7

here until you come back or until Ethan and the others come this way."

"Okay, Cara," Cal said reluctantly. "I'll leave Luke here to protect you." He knew Luke would never leave Cara. He always stayed right beside her. Cal made Cara a hideout among some trees and fixed her a bed made out of leaves. When she was comfortable with her ankle propped up, Cal continued with his scouting, according to plan.

After Cal left, Cara took off her watch and shoes and went to sleep. Luke stood guard beside her.

Cal's scouting turned up no clues. He came back to get Cara, but she and Luke were gone! Cal got very worried and started looking for clues as to where Cara might have gone. He found a moccasin track in the dirt and then he knew… the Comanches had taken her! Cara's watch and shoes were still there where she had slept. Cal also found where Cara had dropped a package of peanut butter crackers to show which direction they took her. According to the tracks, Luke was still with her and he wouldn't let anything happen to her. Since there was no sign of struggle,

Cal figured the Comanches probably just wanted to take her captive. They would have liked seeing Luke's loyalty to her.

"First, I have to tell the others what happened," Cal decided. "Then we have to go find Cara."

Cal went to the meeting place, but no one was there so he kept heading south to find Elyssa and her brothers. He would see if they needed help so they could all go rescue Cara.

Suddenly, Cal saw Gus running toward him. "Did they send you to get us, boy?" Cal asked.

Gus barked and wagged his tail. He turned around, looking back to make sure Cal was following him. Before long, they caught up to Logan, Ethan, and their sister.

"We found Chief Straight Arrow!" Ethan exclaimed. "He fell down into this sink hole. Gus found him, but we can't get him out. The rope in my backpack is too short so we need your rope to tie to it, Cal."

Cal got his rope out of his backpack while explaining what had happened to Cara and Luke.

"When we rescue Chief Straight Arrow, I bet he will make sure Cara and Luke are released," Logan said. "I hope the chief is okay."

The boys tied one end of the rope to a tree and threw the other end down to the Chief, but Straight Arrow didn't come up. While the boys were peering down into the hole, with Ethan shining his flashlight into the darkness, they couldn't see or hear anything down there. When they finally looked up, they saw Chief Straight Arrow and Gus standing by them, looking down into the hole with them. Everyone was shocked to see him there!

"How did you get out?" Elyssa asked the chief.

"Medicine Dog found me. He showed me the way out," said Straight Arrow, pointing at Gus.

"Way to go Gus!" the boys cheered.

They told Straight Arrow about Cara being taken and about the Comanche's impending war on the settlers due to his disappearance.

"While I was going to the settlers' cabins, my pony saw a rattlesnake coming out of that large hole. It spooked him and he threw me," explained Chief Straight Arrow. "I fell down into the hole. It was dark in there, and I could not find a way out! I would have died if you had not brought Medicine Dog to save me. We will not make war with your people. I will get the girl and the dog for you."

They all went to the Comanche camp. The Comanches were amazed to see that Gus, the Spirit Dog with the Ghost-Face, had saved their Chief!

Elyssa and Cara ran to hug each other. "Are you okay, Cara?" Elyssa asked.

"I am now that y'all are here!"

The boys started hugging Cara and the dogs joined in. They were all glad everyone was safe.

The Comanches and settlers became friends again and had a big celebration together at one of the pioneer's cabins. Mr. Hughes played the fiddle while everyone did their own kind of celebration dance. They ate catfish, fried cornbread, corn on the cob, beans, and apple pie. The children dozed off as Chief Straight Arrow chanted the tribal history song and woke up next to the ruins of the pioneer cabin; however, it looked different. There was nothing burned anymore, and it looked like it had just fallen down from age and time.

"Did that really happen or was I dreaming?" asked Cara.

After comparing stories, the children found that they remembered the same things.

"It must have really happened," said Ethan. "See how the cabin just fell down from old age instead of being burned? We prevented the war between the Comanches and the pioneers!"

"I wish we could find some proof," said Logan.

"I've got an idea!" Cal exclaimed. "Let's go to the hideout where I left Cara and look around. Remember, Cara? You left your watch and shoes there."

"I sure did," Cara answered, "and I'd like to have them back!"

"Ethan, Logan, and I will take the dogs there," said Cal. "We'll see if we can dig them up."

Luke was the first to detect something as the boys and dogs started digging for the watch and shoes which Cara had left behind. They found them, but they were in terrible condition since they had been there for 160 years!

"There's your proof, Logan!" Cal declared.

"It sure is!" said Logan. "But I don't think Cara can wear those shoes back to the ranch house."

The boys all laughed. They agreed to take turns carrying Cara piggyback. When they got back to where Cara and Elyssa were waiting for them, Cal said, "Cara, you have the only 160-year-old watch made in the year 2020."

Everyone started laughing.

"What an amazing adventure!" Cara proclaimed, and they all agreed.

Chapter 2

The Lost Canyon

Ethan and Cal had been working hard and playing hard while staying at their grandparents' ranch this summer. They loved every minute of it! The two cousins had helped Grandpa haul hay, pick up rocks out of the field, gather wood, and feed the cows. Since Ethan's dog, Gus, is a cow dog, he helps round up the cows. He gets them out of the brush and thickets so Grandpa can feed them and take care of them.

Cal's dog, Luke, is a Labrador Retriever so he loves finding and retrieving things. The boys throw sticks and floating toys into the creek for Luke to retrieve. Gus retrieves them too, but Luke is a better swimmer.

Every summer, the boys and their dogs have had lots of adventures together. They have made many interesting discoveries on their long hiking expeditions, so Ethan and Cal decided to plan their next hiking trip.

"Let's go hiking to Lost Canyon in the morning, Ethan," Cal suggested.

"Great idea, Cal!" Ethan said. "No one ever goes down there! Maybe we can find some arrowheads to add to our collections."

That night, Grandma fixed the boys and their dogs lots of food and drinks to take with them. Grandpa drew the boys a map to Lost Canyon.

Early the next morning, Ethan, Cal, Gus, and Luke left for their long journey. "If we follow this branch of water which flows into Lucy Creek, we will come to Lost Canyon in a few hours," Ethan explained.

The branch is about two feet deep and crystal clear. It flows all the way from Lost Canyon, where it comes over a waterfall and then runs through the Canyon. There had been a lot of rain, so the boys were looking forward to seeing the waterfall.

Every half hour or so, Ethan and Cal would stop to enjoy the scenery or get snacks or drinks. The dogs would often wade out into the running water to cool off.

After the boys had hiked for hours, Cal said, "This is a long way from civilization. Nothing has changed in this area for hundreds of years!"

"Isn't it awesome to think that all this land used to be inhabited by a band of Comanches?" Cal commented.

"It sure is," Ethan agreed. "Let's look for ancient artifacts! Always look down at the ground for arrowheads while we hike."

By the time the hikers got close to Lost Canyon, they each had found one arrowhead. The arrowheads were made from flint rocks and were perfectly shaped and chipped. Suddenly, Gus and Luke started barking and the boys became worried.

"There may be some predators in the canyon," Ethan suggested. "What is it, boys?"

"I guess your dogs are barking at us," a man said as he came out of hiding. He was holding a pistol and it was aimed at Ethan! Then another man appeared with his gun pointed at Cal. "Call off your dogs!" the first man demanded. The boys calmed the dogs down, but Gus and Luke were still growling low in their throats.

"What are you doing here?" Ethan asked the two men.

"We'll ask the questions!" the first man yelled.

Ethan had to hold Gus back so the dog would not get shot.

"Which way to the highway?" asked one of the men.

"You are miles from any road," Ethan answered. "The county road is about six miles through that thick brush."

"You're going to take us there quick!" The man demanded.

"It's a pretty rough hike. We need to rest first," Ethan said, sounding a lot calmer than he felt.

The second man grabbed Cal's backpack and dug inside. "Look Frank!" The kids have food!"

The two men started devouring the boy's food, but they didn't put their guns down. "Pete, tie the boys' hands and then shoot those dogs!" Frank said.

"Run, Gus! Run, Luke!" the boys yelled. "Go get help!"

Gus and Luke took off on command and the men started shooting at them, but they missed. They dogs were too fast!

"Now you did it!" Frank yelled at the boys. "I might just shoot the both of you!"

"You'll never find your way out of here if you do," Ethan said. "This is called Lost Canyon and if you don't know your way out, YOU will be the ones who are lost!"

"Lead the way, tough guy!" Frank yelled. "Pete, you keep your eye on the other kid and shoot him if he tries to get away!"

"Sure thing, Frank" Pete agreed.

Ethan led the way back up the branch.

"I bet if we just follow this stream, we'll find the road." Frank suggested.

"This stream goes on for miles, but it doesn't go to the road," Cal spoke up. "We have to go through a lot of rough terrain to get out of here. We really better rest for a while."

The men were tired, too, so they all sat down on some big rocks. Even though the men were watching the boys closely, Cal and Ethan were sending secret hand signals to each other behind their backs. The boys had made up their own sign language years ago and always practiced it, but this was the first time they had to use it in a real emergency.

Ethan and Cal had each chosen to sit down on rocks that were close to the thick brush. Cal signaled to Ethan that he should dive in the bushes in three minutes. The boys knew their dogs were still close by even though they told them to go for help. Gus and Luke would not leave the boys when they were in trouble!

After three minutes had passed and the two criminals were relaxing on the rocks, Ethan and Cal yelled, "Now, boys!"

Gus and Luke jumped out of the brush and knocked the guns from the resting men. Cal and Ethan dove into the bushes and crawled to a deer trail they had seen on their way to the canyon. It was far enough away from the branch of water that the two men could probably not find the trail. Then, the boys whistled quietly for their dogs. The men grabbed their guns, but they did not know which direction the boys had gone.

Ethan and Cal, along with the dogs, began to move slowly and stealthily back toward the ranch house. Suddenly, Cal had an idea.

"Ethan, remember that hole Chief Straight Arrow fell into and was trapped in until Gus showed him the way out?"

"Sure, it's not far from here. I know what you're thinking!" Ethan said. "Let's do it!"

The boys soon found the large deep hole. They covered it with long sticks and scattered grass over it so the criminals would not know there was a hole there. Then, Ethan and Cal commanded the dogs to bark. The men heard the dogs. When the boys saw the men coming toward them, they started running away with Gus and Luke. The two men were so intent on chasing the boys, they fell right into the covered hole. They were trapped! The hole had slick rock sides, and no one could climb up out of it. It was about thirty feet deep and pitch-black inside.

Ethan and Cal ran to the ranch house and explained to their grandparents what had happened. Grandpa called Sheriff Jones at once and asked him to come fast. The sheriff brought his deputy and two FBI agents. They explained that these were probably the men that had just robbed the bank in town. When they were trying to escape, the police set up roadblocks, so the men parked their car and escaped on foot.

"The boys can show you where the bank robbers are trapped," Grandpa said. "We have enough horses if you want to ride there. There is no way to drive over that rough terrain."

Ethan and Cal quickly saddled their horses. Sheriff Jones, his Deputy, and the FBI agents also saddled up. The boys and dogs led the way. When they got there, the FBI agent threw down a rope and commanded the two men to climb out. Frank and

Pete refused to come out. They said they would shoot anyone that tried to come down the rope!

"We know a secret way into that hole," Ethan said. "We can get Gus and Luke to go in and get them."

"That sounds like the safest way," the sheriff and FBI agents agreed.

"Go get 'em, boys!" Ethan and Cal yelled.

Gus led the way. Soon, the boys and the officers heard shots coming from down in the hole. The robbers had heard the dogs coming through the secret tunnel and began firing. However, it was so dark that the robbers couldn't see where the dogs were and quickly used up all their bullets. Then, there was a lot of barking, growling, and yelling. Finally, the bank robbers began begging to surrender.

"We can't see anything in here and these dogs are going to tear us apart!" the criminals pleaded.

"Bring 'em out, Gus! They give up!" Ethan commanded.

Gus started herding the criminals out through the secret passage. Luke was behind them, carrying the bag of stolen money in his mouth. Luke took the bag to Cal, who then gave the stolen money to the FBI agent. The sheriff handcuffed the two robbers and told them to walk while everyone else mounted their horses. Gus nipped at the bank robbers' heels, herding them back to the ranch house, and Luke kept up a low, steady growl. Everyone else followed behind on horseback. The FBI agent was amazed at the bravery of the boys and their dogs!

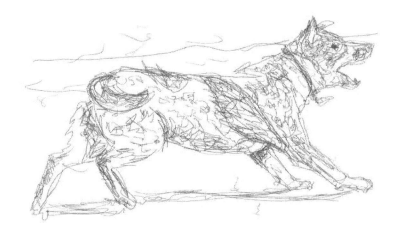

After the criminals were put in the FBI vehicle to be transported to jail, the agent told the boys, "You are going to get a reward for the capture of the bank robbers and the recovery of the stolen money. It looks like I should put your dogs on the payroll."

Everyone laughed. It had been a long, exhausting day, and Ethan and Cal were glad to find out it had been a rewarding one!

Chapter 3

The Great Escape

Ethan, his cousin Cal, and their dogs, Gus and Luke, were eager for some excitement. "Every summer except this one, we have had some great adventures here at the ranch," Ethan told Cal.

"The summer is not over yet," Cal replied. "Let's go on a long hike and see what we can discover!"

"I know the perfect destination," Ethan announced. "Let's go to the Dug Out!"

The boys and their dogs had discovered the Dug Out last summer but hadn't told anyone about it. It was their best-kept secret! Over a hundred years ago, someone had dug a cave out of the side of a hill and made a house out of it. It was back in a remote area on the old Dusty Bales Ranch near Ethan and Cal's grandparents' ranch. Mr. Bales had told the boys they could go exploring on his ranch anytime. He was a good friend of the family and he enjoyed visiting with the boys.

Ethan and Cal got up early the next morning and ate breakfast. Grandma had pancakes, scrambled eggs, and bacon ready for them when they woke up. Grandpa was going to work on his tractor that day, so the boys had the whole day off to go exploring. Grandma fixed them some ham sandwiches, lots of snacks, and drinks. She packed them in each of the boys' backpacks. She also sent food for Gus and Luke.

"Y'all need to be careful and watch out for snakes," Grandma said as always.

"Gus and Luke will also watch for snakes," the boys replied.

As soon as it was daylight, Ethan, Cal, Gus, and Luke started their hike. When the boys discovered the Dug Out last summer, they were amazed at how cool it was. It felt like it was air-conditioned. Since it sat behind a huge Live Oak tree and was dug out from the side of the hill, it had great insulation. There were some old benches, wooden chairs, and a table in it.

"I can't wait to see the Dug Out again," Cal said. "It is so cool there. We can eat our lunch and rest after this long hot hike."

The boys, Gus, and Luke had to go through some thick woods and game trails where it was so dense they had to duck down to follow the path.

"Small animals and deer must have made these trails, and they aren't as tall as we are, so we have to bend down to follow their trails, "Ethan told Cal.

Finally, they came to an opening in the brush. There was a stream with some big rocks next to it.

"Let's eat our lunch here," Ethan suggested. "I don't think I can wait until we reach the Dug Out."

"I'm hungry too!" Cal agreed.

The boys sat on the big rocks and opened their backpacks. The dogs had already jumped in the stream to cool down and get drinks of water. There was a lunch box with an ice pack in it in each boy's backpack. First, Ethan and Cal gave Gus and Luke their dog food. Then the boys ate their ham and cheese sandwiches, potato chips, grapes, and oranges that were already sliced up.

"I'm going to save my apple pie for the Dug Out," said Cal.

Ethan ate his slice of apple pie, but he saved his extra bag of chips and his juice boxes for the Dug Out. They also had extra sandwiches if they got hungry before they got back to the ranch house. Grandma always sent more food than they could eat.

After another hour of hiking, they were almost to the Dug Out when they heard angry voices. Some men were standing in front of the Dug Out with their horses. It sounded like they were arguing.

"Let's get closer and listen," Ethan said. "This doesn't look right."

The boys told their dogs to be quiet and crawled closer. The men raised their voices and the boys could hear them plainly.

"Someone should stay with the old man and make sure he doesn't escape," one of the men demanded.

"We can come right back," the other one said, "but we both need to be at the meeting. That old man can never escape. He is tied up and the door is bolted from the outside. Even if he was able to get out, it's so far from anywhere that he would never make it out of these woods alive." Then the two men mounted their horses and rode away.

"Someone is in big trouble," Ethan and Cal agreed. "We've got to go in and help them."

The boys were able to unbolt the door and open it. Inside, they found Mr. Bales. He was tied up in a chair with his head hanging down. The boys quickly untied him and helped him walk around to get his circulation back.

"Man, am I glad to see y'all!" Mr. Bales cried. "Those men are trying to get me to sign over my ranch to them. I know that if I do, they will kill me so I've been stalling as much as I can. I am very weak right now, and I can't walk very far. Maybe I can hide close by while you go for help."

The boys looked at each other. "Mr. Bales, we have a secret that we discovered last year. It will be the perfect hiding place," explained Ethan.

They showed Mr. Bales a big rock, about five feet tall, at the very back of the Dug Out. There was a hidden metal pin at the top and bottom of the rock. This pin allowed the rock to pivot from side to side.

"Look at this!" Ethan said as he pushed hard on the left side of the rock. The rock slowly swiveled open on the pivot, revealing a hidden room!

"This must have been a secret escape route from the Comanches years ago." Mr. Bales said. "I'm sure there is another way out."

"Yes, there is," answered Ethan. "This room leads into a tunnel. At the end of the tunnel, there is another rock that pivots up and down, and if you push it up from the bottom, you can crawl out. Then, it closes back."

They all went into the secret room and lit a candle that was on a table. Mr. Bales sat down at the table and put his head down. "Boys, those men have not let me have much to eat, and I am weak," he said. Ethan and Cal took out their sandwiches and snacks and let Mr. Bales choose what he wanted.

"This is what I need," Mr. Bales said as he took a box of orange juice and drank it. "I have diabetes and my blood sugar is very low from not eating. This orange juice will raise it quickly."

Soon Mr. Bales was feeling better and was able to eat half a sandwich. "Those men have food stored in the Dug Out," Mr. Bales told the boys.

"I'll go get it and bring it in here," Cal volunteered.

The boys pushed opened the rock door and Cal went back, got all the canned goods, and brought them into the secret room. Cal also found Mr. Bales' insulin for his diabetes and brought it too. There was a trickle of water dripping down the wall of the secret room into a clear pool of water. The overflow ran into a crack below.

"With all this food and water, we could stay here a week," said Cal.

They put the insulin, which was in a waterproof bag, into the pool of water to keep it cool. Then, Mr. Bales explained what had been happening. A group of men had come to his house a few days ago, trying to buy his ranch. Mr. Bales had no intention of selling his ranch and told them so. Then, the men turned mean and roughed him up to try and force him to sign the deed over to them, but he refused.

When they thought Mr. Bales had passed out, they began talking about their plans unaware that Mr. Bales could hear them. He learned that Mr. Potter was a prominent geologist, and he had discovered oil on Mr. Bales' ranch. He had a contract pending with a major oil company to drill for oil, but Mr. Potter needed the title to the ranch and the mineral rights before he could close the deal. He planned on making a fortune since he knew there was a huge oil reserve on Mr. Bales' ranch.

"Excuse me, Sir, but I just want to let you know that my Dad works for a major oil company," Ethan said. "He can help you get a contract with them to drill for oil and make a lot of money, if you want."

"Thank you, Ethan," Mr. Bales said. "After we get out of this trouble, I will talk to your Dad about drilling on my ranch for oil. I'd like to donate a lot of what I make from the oil wells to a foundation which sponsors a program for children that allows them to learn about nature and go camping and hiking, like you boys do each summer."

"That would be a wonderful program!" the boys agreed.

"Maybe the kids could bring their dogs," Ethan suggested.

"Of course, they can," said Mr. Bales. "I will get you and Cal to help me plan the program. But first, we need to plan a way to get out of here."

Mr. Bales then explained what else had happened to him. Mr. Potter had hired some men to help him force Mr. Bales to sign over the deed and then let Mr. Bales die from his diabetes so it would look like natural causes. However, they didn't know that his granddaughter, Rusty, came twice a week to check on Mr. Bales and it was time for her visit.

"I'm worried about Rusty," Mr. Bales said. "She will know something is wrong when she finds those men at my ranch, and I don't know what they will do to her."

"We've got to get her away from them," Ethan said. "I'll go to your ranch house and ask her for a ride home. Then, after we leave, I can explain everything to her."

"That's a good idea," Mr. Bales said. "I've got a bad cut on my arm that I got when those men were trying to force me to sign over my ranch. Ask Rusty if you can borrow my hunting bag. It has a first aid kit in it, and I will need it."

"Okay," Ethan said. "After we get the hunting bag, we'll come back here and get you, Cal, and Luke. Gus will come with me."

"Luke and I will take care of Mr. Bales until y'all get back," said Cal. "Good luck!"

Ethan and Gus went through the tunnel, pushed up the rock exit, and crawled through it as it closed behind them. Ethan made sure to cover up the opening with brush after he got out and wipe out all the tracks away with a cedar branch. They rushed to Mr. Bales' ranch house as fast as they could and arrived just as Rusty was driving up. Unfortunately, the men were coming out of the ranch house at the same time, so Ethan didn't get to talk to Rusty first.

"Hello, Ethan and Gus," Rusty said, smiling. She patted Gus on the head.

Mr. Potter came out to meet Rusty and said, "Hello, you just missed Mr. Bales. He went into town with my partner, but they will be coming right back."

Rusty was immediately suspicious. "Why would he leave? My grandfather knows I always come out on Wednesdays to cook and clean for him. Who are you, and what are you doing here?"

"We are old friends of Mr. Bales and are staying with him for a couple of days," said Mr. Potter. "We are going to take him fishing in the morning. My name is Mr. Potter."

"I haven't heard him mention you before, Mr. Potter," said Rusty. "I will wait right here until my grandfather gets back."

Ethan then spoke up. "Rusty, your grandfather told me I could borrow his hunting bag whenever I needed it. I came all this way to borrow it. Can you please get it for me and give me a ride home? I am too tired to hike back, and it will be dark before I can get back to the ranch."

Rusty looked at Mr. Potter. "When I come back, my grandfather better be all right," she said.

"Of course, why wouldn't he be?" said Mr. Potter, acting offended.

Rusty went into the house and got the hunting bag out of the closet. Then she, Ethan, and Gus got in her car and backed out of the drive.

"Rusty," Ethan whispered, "We've got to be careful. We need to get away from these men so we can get help for your grandfather."

Rusty stayed calm and asked, "What has happened to him, Ethan?"

Ethan began to explain the situation.

"My cell phone doesn't get any signal out here so I can't call for help until we get closer to town," Rusty said.

They were about to cross the cattle guard when two men with guns stopped them. "Get out of the car!" the men yelled.

Rusty stepped on the gas and tried to get past them. The two men started shooting at the car! They shot the tires out so Rusty swerved into the bushes. She, Ethan, and Gus jumped out of the car and dove into the brush. Ethan remembered to grab the hunting bag right before he jumped. The men kept shooting, but Rusty, Ethan, and Gus kept moving as fast as they could, and the bullets missed them. They heard the men saying that they were going to get their bloodhounds to track them and that the dogs would take care of them.

"Don't worry Rusty," Ethan said. "Your grandfather is safe with Cal and Luke and we can get to them in about thirty minutes if we hurry."

They took the shortest route to the Dug Out and the Secret Room. They had to cross through some thick brush, canyons and creeks; but fortunately, Rusty was in good shape since she was on the tennis team in college. She had beautiful long dark red hair so Rusty was the perfect name for her.

Finally, they made it back to the Dug Out. Ethan pushed the big rock and when it pivoted open, Rusty was amazed to see the Secret Room. When they went into the room, Rusty was relieved to see her grandfather, but she was also concerned about him.

"I've never seen him so sick and weak," she said.

"He's been badly treated these last few days," Cal replied. "We need to get him to a doctor."

Ethan took the first aid kit out of the hunting bag. Rusty knew what to do since she was studying to be a registered nurse. First, she had to stitch Mr. Bales' arm. It required seven stitches. Then, she checked his blood sugar with the monitor that was in the first aid kit and found that his blood glucose level was dangerously low.

"We have some more orange juice boxes," Cal said. He opened one and gave it to Mr. Bales. Then Rusty got him to eat a little more of a sandwich and soon he was feeling much stronger.

"We heard those men say they were going to get their bloodhounds to track us," Ethan advised.

Mr. Bales sat up. "Boys, I've got some skunk scent in the hunting bag. I use it when I am hunting to cover my scent. If y'all pour it out at the opening, it may stop the dogs from smelling us. Also, be sure and wipe out any tracks in front of the opening."

Ethan and Cal each grabbed a bottle of skunk scent, pushed the rock open, and crawled through. After they sprinkled the skunk scent around the rock passage, they brushed away the footprints with a broken tree branch. Then the boys poured the skunk scent in front of the rock opening and put some on the swiveling rock as well. They were careful not to touch the rock with their backs when they crawled back under it. When Ethan and Cal came back into the Secret Room, Rusty smiled at them.

"Y'all smell a little bit like skunks yourselves, but I don't mind," she said. "You are both my heroes!"

When Mr. Potter went to the Dug Out and found Mr. Bales gone, he began to worry.

"Those dogs need to find that girl and boy," he told the other men. "They must have found her grandfather."

The bloodhounds were barking and growling outside of the opening, but they soon left.

"The skunk scent worked!" Rusty said. "But we've got to get help!"

"We forgot about our walkie-talkies!" Cal exclaimed. "Grandma always puts them in our backpacks and keeps one with her at the ranch house in case of an emergency."

The boys took out their walkie-talkies, but they wouldn't transmit inside the cavern.

"We've got to get out and get a message to Grandma," Cal said. "We can take Gus and Luke with us in case the bloodhounds come while we're out there."

The boys crawled out under the rock opening and held the rock open for the dogs to come through. Unfortunately, both dogs rubbed their backs on the rock where the skunk scent was. Then the boys hurried up the nearby hill until the walkie-talkies began to transmit. They called Grandma and she answered at once.

"Where are you?" she asked.

Ethan explained the situation as concisely as possible. He told her where the Dug Out was and about the men and dogs at Mr. Bales' ranch. He also told her that Mr. Bales needed medical attention. Then, he signed off.

Suddenly, the boys heard the bloodhounds coming in the distance. They began running back to the secret opening. It didn't look like they were going to make it before the bloodhounds attacked!

Gus and Luke ran toward the bloodhounds, growling and snarling, with the hair on their backs standing straight up. They charged at the bloodhounds and the dogs began fighting. Gus and Luke were fighting for their lives to protect Ethan and Cal! The boys made it to the rock opening. They called their dogs, but they couldn't get away from the bloodhounds.

"We're sorry boys, but we have to leave you on your own for now," said Cal.

Ethan and Cal made it through the rock opening and dropped the rock back down. Then they put another rock in front of the opening so it could not be opened from the outside. They went back into the room where Rusty and Mr. Bales were.

"We got the message through to Grandma. She and Grandpa will know what to do," the boys informed them.

"I am so thankful. Grandpa Bales needs medical attention, but I know he will be okay now," said Rusty.

Soon helicopters from the Department of Public Safety and Emergency Medical Services landed near the Dug Out. The Sheriff, Grandpa, and some troopers came into the Dug Out and found Mr. Potter and his men there. Ethan could see into the Dug Out from a small hole in the wall between the Dug Out and the Secret Room. He heard Mr. Potter telling the Sheriff that he and his men were looking for Mr. Bales because he had wandered off, and they were worried about him.

"Help has arrived!" Ethan told the others as he pushed open the rock door.

Rusty ran through. "Arrest these men!" she told the officers. "They kidnapped my grandfather and tried to kill us!"

The troopers read Mr. Potter and his men their rights and put them in handcuffs. Ethan and Cal started explaining everything to Grandpa and Sheriff Jones.

"We're got to find Gus and Luke! They may need help," the boys pleaded.

Rusty went in the EMS Helicopter with her grandfather, and the boys went in the DPS helicopter with Grandpa and Sheriff Jones. As they left, the helicopters shone their spotlight all around the area where the dogs had been fighting but saw nothing.

"We've got to head back and get these men booked into jail," the pilot told the boys. "We can come back and look for the dogs tomorrow when it is daylight."

Ethan and Cal were worried about Gus and Luke.

"That was a vicious dog fight," said Ethan. "Our dogs are probably hurt and need our help."

"They'll be okay," Grandpa said reassuringly. "I'm just glad nothing happened to y'all, thanks to Gus and Luke!"

The helicopter landed and dropped Grandpa and the boys off close to the ranch house. Just before they landed, they received a message that Mr. Bales was going to be fine. Grandma ran out to meet them.

After the helicopter left and Grandma quit hugging Ethan and Cal, they all started walking to the front porch. "I smell a skunk!" Cal exclaimed.

Then, they saw Gus and Luke crashed out on the front porch. The boys started hugging their dogs. They were never so happy to smell a skunk!

Please share this book with your friends and family
and post a review on Amazon!

http://www.amazon.com/author/mitchellsusan

Made in the USA
Middletown, DE
13 October 2021